MICHAEL DAHL **PRESENTS**
SCARY STORIES

REVENGE OF THE KRAKEN

BY MEGAN ATWOOD

ILLUSTRATED BY NEIL EVANS

STONE ARCH BOOKS
a capstone imprint

Published by Stone Arch Books, an imprint of Capstone
1710 Roe Crest Drive
North Mankato, Minnesota 56003
capstonepub.com

Library of Congress Cataloging-in-Publication Data
Names: Atwood, Megan, author. | Evans, Neil, illustrator.
Title: Revenge of the Kraken / by Megan Atwood ; illustrated by Neil Evans.
Description: North Mankato, Minnesota : Stone Arch Books, an imprint of
   Capstone, [2022] | Series: Michael Dahl presents: scary stories |
   Audience: Ages 8–11. | Audience: Grades 4–6. | Summary: Jordan tries to
   follow his grandpa's example and treat the sea with respect, but he is
   unable to stop his friends' father from trying to hunt an endangered
   dolphin who unbeknownst to them is protected by the Kraken!
Identifiers: LCCN 2021002630 (print) | LCCN 2021002631 (ebook) |
   ISBN 9781663911315 (hardcover) | ISBN 9781663911285 (ebook pdf)
Subjects: CYAC: Sea stories—Fiction. | Grandfathers—Fiction. |
   Kraken—Fiction. | Horror stories.
Classification: LCC PZ7.A8952 Re 2022 (print) | LCC PZ7.A8952 (ebook) | DDC
   [Fic]—dcundefined
LC record available at https://lccn.loc.gov/2021002630
LC ebook record available at https://lccn.loc.gov/2021002631

Designed by Kay Fraser

Printed and bound in the USA.   4270

MICHAEL
DAHL
PRESENTS

Michael Dahl has written about werewolves, magicians, and superheroes. He loves funny books, scary books, and mysterious books. Every Michael Dahl Presents book is chosen by Michael himself and written by an author he loves. The books are about favorite subjects like monster aliens, haunted houses, farting pigs, or magical powers that go haywire. Read on!

SHARE THE FEAR!

You are not alone. And I don't mean that a creature
lurks in the dark shadows of your bedroom. Or a slimy
menace lives under your bed. (Although that might
be true.) I mean, you are not alone in being afraid.
Everyone is afraid of something. Every. Single. Person.
Reading about other people's fears in these weird tales,
you might learn how to overcome your own.
Or you might learn how to escape from zombie teachers
attacking the school. Both are good things to know.
Just be sure to leave the lights on while reading!

Michael Dahl

TABLE OF CONTENTS

Chapter 1

THE SEA-CRET KEEPER

"It's just a few months, that's all," Jordan's mom said. "Your dad and I just need the summer alone to talk about things."

She tried to straighten Jordan's shirt, but he backed up and pushed her hands away. He was twelve—not a baby. He glanced around the street of the small coastal town of Cape May to see if anyone had noticed. But it was just him and his parents, standing outside his grandpa's small, run-down house.

He wasn't a baby, but Jordan already felt homesick thinking about a summer without his parents or friends—stuck in the small house with his grandpa, Captain Joe. So what if it was across from the beach. There would be no pickup basketball games, no video games with his friends.

Jordan's dad ruffled his already messy, brown hair. "You'll have fun, kiddo," he said. "Who doesn't want to be by the beach all summer? Maybe you can learn how to surf. Or Grandpa will teach you how to work his boat. He knows a lot about the ocean, you know. People used to come to ask him all of their seafaring questions."

As if they'd summoned him, Captain Joe opened the door and grunted at them. Jordan was tall for his age, but his grandpa towered over him. He wore a boat captain's hat and gray hair poked out from the sides and back of it. He and his grandpa seemed to have messy hair in common, anyway.

"Well, don't stand there all day," Captain Joe said. "Get inside."

They walked in and Jordan got a whiff of the house. It smelled musty and briny. Hardly any light made it inside and there were things piled everywhere.

His grandpa turned to Jordan's parents. He rubbed his white and gray, scruffy stubble. He studied them with blue, twinkly eyes. "Well, you staying or going?"

Jordan's mom laughed. "We'll let Jordan get settled." She turned to Jordan, and he tried hard not to cry. He looked down and refused to look her in the eyes.

"It's just for a few months. We'll call you every day," his mom whispered. She wrapped him in a hug, and he tried hard not to cling. When she was done, his dad hugged him.

His voice was gruff. "Do as Captain Joe says. Love ya, kiddo."

Jordan mumbled, "Love you too," to both his parents.

Captain Joe hugged Jordan's mom and gave his dad a hearty handshake. "I'll look after the boy. Don't you worry," he said.

Jordan tried hard not to take that as a threat.

He watched as his parents walked out the door and abandoned him. They waved as they left, and Jordan's stomach sank.

It was real. They were really leaving him here. And he hadn't said a word to stop them.

When he turned around, his grandpa was sizing him up with one squinty eye.

"Let's take a walk, kid. You can get to know the place a little," he said. He looked Jordan up and down. "I'll need to feed you more, too, to get some meat on your bones. You'll need good muscles on the boat. Pump up those skinny little legs." Captain Joe didn't wait for Jordan to follow. He just adjusted his hat and walked out the door. Jordan scrambled after him.

They walked across the street to the Cape May boardwalk. Jordan had to practically run to keep up with him. But soon he found the rhythm and was able to take in the scenery. Seagulls circled overhead, squawking. The roar of the ocean drowned out nearly everything else. But Jordan found he loved the sounds and the smell in the air.

A young couple walked past them on the boardwalk. Both of them nodded at his grandpa and said, "Captain." Everyone they passed, in fact, nodded and called him Captain. It seemed as if he knew the whole town.

They walked until they came to a marina where a bunch of boats were docked. Captain Joe led Jordan to a relatively small boat. It looked old but clean and sturdy. The name *The Sea-cret Keeper* was on the back. On the dock next to it was a sign that said, *Tours: $20 for one hour.*

"This here is my beauty," said Captain Joe. "She's been my boat for more than thirty years now. Both she and the sea have been very good to me. If you respect things, they will respect you back."

Something shiny to the left caught Jordan's eye. A much larger, newer boat sat at the dock next to Captain Joe's. On its back end was the name *The Dream Maker.* A huge arch on the dock next to the boat had the words, *Make Your*

Dreams Come True! across it. A sign tacked on the arch said, *Guided Tour and More! $50.*

Captain Joe saw where Jordan was looking and scowled. "Yeah, *The Dream Maker* sure looks fancy," he said. "But the owner does some pretty awful things. Fishing for endangered species. Thinking he owns the ocean. Nothing good will come of that, mark my words."

Jordan brought his gaze back to *The Sea-cret Keeper.* "What secrets does your boat keep?"

Captain Joe threw back his head and laughed. "Stick with me, kid, and I'll let you in on a few of them." His eyes twinkled and his whole face lit up.

Jordan grinned as they continued their walking tour of the harbor. Maybe this wouldn't be the worst summer after all.

Chapter 2

NEW FRIENDS

The next morning, Jordan woke up to an empty house. A note left on the cluttered table said, *Cereal in cupboard. Milk in fridge. Got a tour to do—go explore and come back for lunch. Your mom told me to tell you to put on sunscreen.*

Jordan couldn't believe it. His parents hardly ever let him do stuff by himself. But after he got dressed, ate breakfast, and put on sunscreen, he wasn't sure where to start. Finally, he decided to go to the boardwalk and head the opposite direction from which he and Captain Joe had walked the night before.

The boardwalk was busy! The temperature had spiked, and it seemed like everyone had decided to hang out at the beach. Jordan walked for about a half a mile when he spotted some basketball courts in the distance. He could see kids playing and his heart soared. He tried not to get too excited. They could be way older than him. Still, he hurried along until he was right next to the courts.

Two boys, who were obviously brothers, played one-on-one. Jordan thought they were probably about his age. He stood awkwardly by the courts, watching, not sure how to introduce himself. Turned out he didn't have to.

"Hey!" said one of the boys. "Want to play HORSE?"

Jordan grinned. "Yeah. I'm in!"

For the next hour and a half, Jordan played hard. He couldn't quit smiling. He missed his friends, but these guys seemed cool. His new summer friends were twins named Derek and Tyler, and they were pretty good at basketball.

Jordan checked his watch—it was almost time for lunch.

"I have to walk back to my grandpa's," he said.

"If you're going that way, we'll walk with you," said Derek. He pointed the way Jordan had come. "Our dad's down that way. He owns *The Dream Maker*."

They started walking, Tyler bouncing the ball every other step.

"Oh, I saw your boat!" Jordan said. "My grandpa owns *The Sea-cret Keeper*. It's right next to yours."

Derek and Tyler shared a look and snorted. "Your grandpa is Captain Joe? Are you staying with him all summer?"

Jordan wasn't sure what was so funny. "Yeah," he said uncertainly.

"Good luck with that!" Tyler said, and the twins dissolved into laughter. Jordan frowned.

Derek looked up. "Oh, sorry, man," he said. "It's just the captain is always going on about treating the sea with respect, blah blah blah. We just think he's funny, that's all. Plus his boat is so tiny."

They were almost to his grandpa's house, and Jordan slowed down. He laughed uneasily. "I don't really know him that well," he said. He stopped in front of the house.

"Well, don't worry," Tyler said. "We'll hang out with you. You can just stick with us this summer. We'll grab you tomorrow, okay?"

He threw the ball at Derek and then started running down the boardwalk, bumping into people. "Over here, Derek!" he yelled.

Derek grinned and took off after him, leaving Jordan to think about his new friends.

Chapter 3

GODDESS OF THE SEA

After lunch, Captain Joe took Jordan to *The Sea-cret Keeper*. He pointed to the front of the boat. "Bow," he said. Then he pointed to the back. "Stern."

Then his grandpa pointed to the right side of the boat and said, "Starboard." Then the left, "Port. Get to know these terms—if you're going to be my first mate, you should know a thing or two."

Jordan smiled to himself. He liked the idea of being first mate. He put on his life jacket and then climbed into the boat, practicing the new terms under his breath.

Captain Joe climbed in and untied the rope. He started the engine and then winked at Jordan. His whole face had changed—now he glowed with happiness. Gone was the gruff and grumpy guy he seemed to be.

"Ready?" his grandpa asked, winking again and grinning. Jordan grinned back and nodded. Captain Joe pushed the throttle, and Jordan felt the first spray of the ocean.

The wind whipped through his hair as the boat sped forward. Jordan couldn't remember feeling happier. Being on the boat felt like flying. Captain Joe pointed and shouted something that Jordan couldn't hear. But he followed the captain's finger and saw a pod of dolphins leaping in the air not too far away from them. Jordan's face hurt from smiling so much.

When they were far enough out in the ocean that Jordan could barely see land, Captain Joe cut the engine.

"What do you think, kid?" he asked Jordan.

"This is awesome!" Jordan practically yelled.

Captain Joe laughed and sat down across from him. "Can't say I mind it myself," he said.

His grandpa leaned down and opened a tiny, beat-up-looking cooler under his seat. He grabbed a soda and handed it to Jordan.

"I've been sailing since I was your age," Captain Joe said. "First was sailboats. Then I got this beaut when I was in my twenties. I've seen some things on these seas, let me tell you. Things can go south quicker than a blink of an eye. But if you pay attention and take care of the sea, she'll take care of you."

"What things have you seen?" Jordan asked. The waves rocked the boat, and the breeze blew gently against him. Jordan could still see the dolphins playing nearby.

"Hmm. Let me tell you a little about the ocean here," Captain Joe said. Jordan settled back against the seat and took a sip of his soda.

"The sea is a fickle thing, and she demands respect," his grandpa continued. "Our job is to protect her—we make sure she's taken care of, and that her creatures are honored. These new young outfits, like *The Dream Maker*, they come out here and they fish for things they have no business fishing for. I've made quite an enemy of them and others, speaking out against their practices. But the measure of a person is standing up and speaking up for what's right. Mark my words, son, if they keep up that foolishness, the sea will have its revenge."

Jordan thought about how the boys he had met laughed about Captain Joe. And Jordan hadn't said anything. He looked down and took another sip of his soda to hide his shame.

"Psst. Kid. Look over there," Captain Joe suddenly whispered.

Jordan looked to where the captain was pointing, wondering why he was whispering all of a sudden. At first he saw nothing. Then he saw a beautiful white dolphin leaping out of the water next to them, so close Jordan could almost touch her.

"It's Tia," Captain Joe said quietly. Jordan thought he saw a tear in his eye. "That's Tiamat, the goddess of the ocean. She's come to say hi!"

Captain Joe smiled broadly. He went into the engine cabin and played a special horn. The dolphin leaped and then spun in the air before splashing down.

Jordan laughed and Captain Joe whooped, being his loud self again.

"I play that horn especially for her!" his grandpa said.

"I've never seen a white dolphin before," Jordan said. "She's beautiful!" Just as the words left his lips, Tia leaped and spun again. Then she stood up on her tail. Jordan laughed with glee.

"This here is a real honor. This is why we take care of the ocean. Look at that beauty," Captain Joe said.

With a flick of her tail, Tia sped toward them and leaped all around the boat. Jordan thought he might have a little tear in his eye too. He'd never seen anything so wonderful. Then as fast as she'd come, Tia disappeared. Jordan and Captain Joe shared a look and a smile.

"Well, I think that's as good as it's going to get, " Captain Joe said. "Might as well call it a day." He pushed the button to pull up the boat's anchor.

"That there was the goddess of the ocean, sure as I'm living and breathing, Jordan." Captain Joe looked him in the eye. "Legend has it when Tia is feeling good, the ocean is good. But if Tia doesn't like something, or if she's threatened . . . the other part of the ocean comes alive. And that's one part you don't ever want to meet."

"What part?" Jordan asked.

Captain Joe's eyes darkened.

"The Kraken," he said. "If Tia wants revenge, she sends the Kraken. And nothing will save you then."

His grandpa started the engine and Jordan got a chill. He didn't want to meet that part of the ocean either. He hoped he never would.

Chapter 4

NOT QUITE A DREAM

The next morning, Jordan still felt elated from the boat ride the day before. He wanted to ask his grandpa if he could join him on his tours and learn more about the ocean. But before he could, someone knocked on the door.

"I'll get it," Jordan said. Captain Joe grunted.

When Jordan opened the door, Derek and Tyler stood on the step. They craned their necks to peek around Jordan and see inside the house, but he blocked their view.

"Hey," Tyler said. "We wanted to know if you could come hang out with us today."

Jordan felt a thrill—even though he wasn't totally sure about them yet. Still, they were his age. And they liked basketball. He felt Captain Joe come up behind him.

"Derek. Tyler," Captain Joe said. "Your father doing alright, I gather?"

"Yessir," Derek said. Jordan thought he saw a little smirk.

"Can I hang out with them?" Jordan asked.

His grandpa tightened his lips. "Do what you want. Just be back for dinner," he said as he walked away, leaving Jordan uncertain in the doorway.

"Come on," Tyler said. "We're going to have fun." He and Derek turned away, and Jordan took one last look at his grandpa before shutting the door and following them.

Once they reached the boardwalk, Jordan asked, "What do you want to do today?"

"Do you want to see our boat?" Derek asked. "It's just up ahead."

Jordan perked up. "Yeah! I went out on my grandpa's boat yesterday. It was pretty awesome."

"That old thing?" Tyler said. "Wait until you see ours."

They reached the dock where *The Dream Maker* sat. Jordan once again felt impressed by how big and shiny it was. A man climbed up on deck wearing a red polo shirt and khakis. He ran a hand through his glossy hair.

"You must be Joe's grandson, huh? He's quite a guy." The man shared a look with Derek and Tyler. "I'm Mr. Paxton, Derek and Tyler's dad. Why don't you climb on up here to see how a real boat runs."

Jordan didn't like the way they all talked about his grandpa. But he really wanted to see what *The Dream Maker* was like. So he followed Derek and Tyler onto the deck and put on his life jacket. He and Derek and Tyler sat in some fancy bucket seats next to each other.

"You're in for a real treat, boys. If we've timed it right, you'll get to see something pretty amazing soon," Mr. Paxton said. He turned on the boat's engine, and Derek and Tyler slapped a high five. Jordan smiled and high fived them too. Maybe he should relax a little. His grandpa did take a little getting used to, he had to admit.

The boat sped off into the waves, knocking hard against them. Jordan had to hold onto his seat so he wasn't bounced off. He couldn't believe how fast they were going. This didn't feel anything like yesterday—the wind whipped against his face and the water sprayed up at

him so hard that it stung his cheeks. Derek and Tyler seemed to be having the time of their lives though. They laughed hysterically through the whole thing.

"Isn't this awesome?" Tyler yelled. Jordan tried to smile and nod. But his stomach felt a little sick.

Finally the boat slowed down and Jordan could hear again. The engine still ran but it was low now, with the boat barely moving forward.

"Okay, boys, keep your eyes open. We're looking for a white dolphin," Mr. Paxton said as he moved toward the front of the boat—the bow, as Jordan knew it now. "I saw her a while back so I know she's here. And I also know she'll look fantastic on my mantelpiece."

"Yes!" Derek and Tyler said at the same time and moved to the sides of the boat, looking over the edges.

Jordan wasn't sure he'd heard Mr. Paxton correctly. He moved over to where Tyler was leaning over.

"What did your dad say?" Jordan asked quietly.

"He's going to hunt a white dolphin! It'll go up on the wall, just like his other trophies. A great hammerhead shark. A leatherback turtle. He collects endangered species," Tyler said with excitement.

"Ahem. I 'accidentally' got those as trophies," Mr. Paxton said, using his fingers to make air quotes. "Just like I'm going to *accidentally* get that white dolphin." He winked at Jordan. "Don't tell your grandpa! He gets all worked up about these things."

Now Jordan really did feel sick. Before he could say anything, Derek yelled, "Dad! Over there!"

To Jordan's horror, Tia swam just a few yards away, leaping through the water and doing her flips. Jordan knew he should say something. He couldn't let this happen.

But when he tried to speak, nothing came out of his mouth.

Mr. Paxton raised a deadly looking harpoon gun and aimed. Tia swam closer, slowing down. Jordan wanted to yell at her to SWIM AWAY! But still no words came out. Jordan's eyes filled with tears.

"Stay right there, you magnificent creature," Mr. Paxton said softly. As his finger tightened on the trigger, Jordan did the only thing he could think of. He pretended to trip right into Mr. Paxton.

Mr. Paxton shot right when Jordan bumped into him, and the harpoon went wide. Still, Jordan watched helplessly as the harpoon

skimmed Tia, leaving a long, angry red mark on her back. Tia stopped and looked at them.

"I'm sorry," Jordan mouthed. Then Tia dove under the water.

"Dang it!" Mr. Paxton said, dropping the harpoon gun. "Now she'll dive down and we won't see her again for days. Maybe not ever."

"Sorry, Mr. Paxton," Jordan said—not meaning it one bit and trying not to smile. Derek and Tyler gave him dirty looks, but Jordan felt nothing but relieved that Tia had gotten away.

"It's fine," Mr. Paxton said, though it looked like it pained him. "There's always another day. Might as well head back since this trip has been wasted."

Jordan couldn't agree more. He wanted nothing more than to be back at his grandpa's.

Chapter 5

THE NIGHTMARE MAKER

That night, Jordan couldn't sleep. He kept replaying the scene where Tia almost got harpooned. He kept wondering why he hadn't said anything. His grandpa's words echoed in his head: *The measure of a person is standing up and speaking up for what's right.*

When he got up in the morning, he'd made up his mind. He was going to tell Mr. Paxton that what he did was wrong. And he was going to tell Derek and Tyler that his grandpa was one of the coolest guys he'd ever met.

After making the decision, Jordan couldn't keep still. Sitting at the breakfast table, he kept looking at the door and fidgeting, anxious to get going and make things right.

Captain Joe eyed Jordan's bouncing knee. "You look like you have some things to say," he said.

Jordan swallowed. He couldn't get up the nerve to tell him what happened. He had to say his piece to Mr. Paxton and the boys first. So he just shook his head.

The captain looked at him for a minute longer, then nodded. "All right then," he said. "I'll be leading a tour in a bit. The water is looking a little restless today. I want to get the tourists in and out before she takes a turn for the worse. Will you be joining me?"

Jordan swallowed his cereal. "Can I join you after your first run?" he asked.

"If that's what you want, son," Captain Joe replied.

Jordan nodded and got up. "I just have to do something first." He walked to the door and turned to wave at his grandpa.

"I hope you can ease whatever is troubling you," Captain Joe said.

Jordan nodded. He intended to. He stood tall and walked out the door.

Walking quickly to the boardwalk, Jordan noticed that the sea really did seem restless. The waves were rolling steadily, and the sky was turning gray. He hurried up to where *The Dream Maker* sat, hoping to see Mr. Paxton and maybe the boys. Jordan glanced longingly at *The Sea-cret Keeper*, silently promising the boat he'd see her later.

Suddenly, the engine of *The Dream Maker* started, and Jordan turned to watch as Derek and Tyler popped up from the cabin. Tyler moved to untie the boat.

"Tyler!" Jordan yelled. Tyler and Derek both looked at him, and Mr. Paxton walked out of the engine cabin. Jordan's throat almost closed up, but he gathered his courage. "Mr. Paxton, I need to talk to you!"

Mr. Paxton looked irritated, and Tyler and Derek rolled their eyes at each other. Jordan tried to calm the butterflies in his stomach.

"Well, this boat is leaving right now, so if you want to talk, you better climb on board. But this time, maybe try not to be so clumsy," Mr. Paxton said, smiling. Jordan noticed his smile didn't reach his eyes.

Jordan was torn. He wanted to get this over with but didn't want to be stuck on their boat. Then he remembered that his grandpa had also said that the job of people was to take care of the ocean. And, clearly, Mr. Paxton did anything but that.

So Jordan squared his shoulders and hopped on the boat. Tyler untied the rope and—just as Jordan snapped on his life jacket—Mr. Paxton pushed the throttle hard. The boat jumped forward.

For the second time in two days, Jordan had to hold on tight and try to keep his food down. When the boat finally slowed, Jordan had to swallow several times to calm his roiling stomach.

The engine purred in the background as Mr. Paxton came out of the engine cabin and looked through a pair of binoculars. Without saying anything, Tyler and Derek took places at starboard and port to look over the ocean.

Jordan knew they were looking for Tia. He had to say something.

He cleared his throat. He started, "It . . . was wrong," he mumbled.

"Mm-hmm. That's okay, Jordan," Mr. Paxton said distractedly. "We're going to try again today."

Jordan cleared his throat again. "What you're doing is wrong, Mr. Paxton!" he said, louder than he intended.

Mr. Paxton put down the binoculars and narrowed his eyes. He smirked. "Ahh. So your grandpa got to you, huh? Well, I don't have time for that old-fashioned nonsense. I take what I want, when I want it," he said, putting the binoculars up to his eyes again.

Tyler snickered.

"You're a weirdo, just like your grandpa," Derek said under his breath.

Anger coursed through Jordan.

"Captain Joe is the best grandpa and the best boat captain, and he knows more about this ocean than anyone. He says our job is to protect it, not ruin it!" Jordan realized he was yelling, but he didn't care.

Before anyone could respond, Tyler yelled, "Dad! Starboard!"

Jordan's stomach sank. That could only mean Tia. He looked starboard and, sure enough, there was Tia, skimming the water. For the first time since being on the boat, though, Jordan noticed how much rougher the waves were getting. The sky had darkened even more, taking on an evil grayish-green color. The water started to buck the boat up and down.

The next few things happened so fast, Jordan could barely process them. Mr. Paxton whooped with glee and dropped the binoculars. Then he lunged for his harpoon gun at the same time as Jordan. They both got a hold of it.

At the exact same moment, Tyler yelled, "DAD! It's not alone!"

The fear in Tyler's voice made Jordan turn toward Tia. Mr. Paxton did too. Then they both dropped the harpoon.

Tia swam around something churning in the water. Something so big, it made a large, swirling whirlpool. As Jordan watched, a huge tentacle—easily longer than two football fields—shot out of the water. Then another. Then another.

Then a great, big, orange eye surfaced and looked right at Jordan.

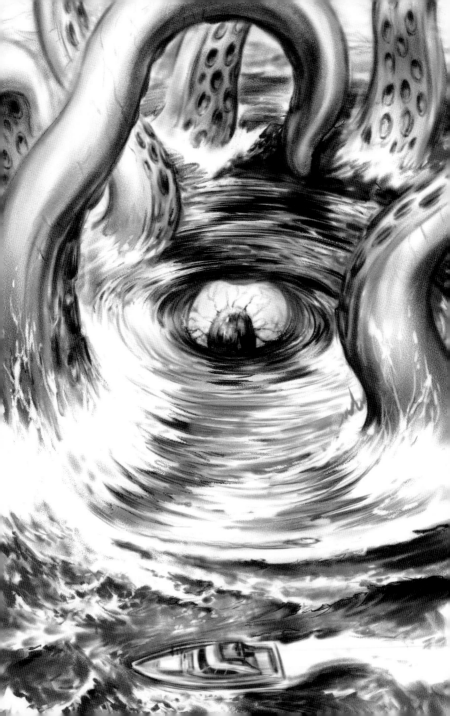

Chapter 6

WRAPPED IN TERROR

Jordan's knees buckled. This had to be the sea monster his grandpa had warned him about.

The Kraken.

"Dad?" Derek said, his voice trembling. But Mr. Paxton was already moving. He sprinted to the engine cabin. He grabbed the radio and yelled, "MAYDAY, MAYDAY" into it.

Only static came back at him. Then a string of garbled words.

The sky thundered and the clouds above them began to circle, mirroring the whirlpool in the water that was starting to pull the boat toward it. Jordan knew if they didn't move soon, they'd be sucked down into the water, right next to the monster.

"Sit down, boys!" Mr. Paxton yelled. "We're in for a bumpy ride!"

Jordan didn't have to be told twice and quickly took a seat. Mr. Paxton pushed the throttle, and the boat made a grinding noise. Grunting and pulling at the wheel, he strained to turn the boat around. When they were finally pointed toward land, the boat shuddered and groaned before finally jumping forward, breaking free from the whirlpool's suction.

Jordan wanted to whoop, but the dark skies and the tentacles above him meant they were still in big trouble. The boat continued to make grinding noises, but Jordan could feel it start to gain some speed.

Then, as quickly as it had jumped forward, the boat stopped. All at once, it tilted portside.

Jordan clung to his seat, holding on tight so he wouldn't be dumped into the water. As the boat kept tipping, he realized what was happening: A tentacle had suctioned itself to the side of the vessel. In his position, Jordan could see many more tentacles writhing beneath the water.

As he hung on, Jordan felt a rush of air above him, and he looked up. His jaw dropped open. He watched in horror as a tentacle sped toward them. In one quick move, it slammed down in the middle of the boat, sending Jordan flying—and screaming—through the air.

Jordan landed in the ocean with a splat, dipping below the churning water before his

life jacket pulled him back up. He sputtered as he broke the surface, trying to clear his eyes of saltwater.

Underneath him, Jordan could feel the creature's other wriggling tentacles. He looked around for Mr. Paxton and the boys, but he couldn't see them anywhere.

But then Jordan realized he could hear them. The roar of the ocean almost drowned them out, but he definitely heard screaming. It sounded like it was coming from . . . above?

Jordan looked up. Three tentacles waved in the air, each one holding a person. The huge sea monster had curled its tentacles around Mr. Paxton, Derek, and Tyler.

A tentacle neared Jordan, and he tried to swim away. But even with the roiling of the ocean, he could feel the tentacle closing in. Jordan felt like he was swimming through quicksand and his muscles ached. He could barely breathe. He felt the surge of the ocean beneath him, and something touched his ankle, then slowly wrapped around it. This was it. The monster had him. The tentacle started to drag him under.

Chapter 7

THE MOST BEAUTIFUL SOUND

Jordan held his breath, waiting to be pulled to his death. But just then, he heard the most beautiful sound he'd ever heard in his life.

His grandpa's boat horn, playing the tune just for Tia.

Jordan watched as *The Sea-cret Keeper* zeroed in on him. But it was too late—the monster tugged and pulled him under. Jordan tried to fight, but it was no use. The monster was way too strong.

Just as his lungs were about to burst, Jordan was suddenly launched straight into the sky. He took a huge gulp of air and realized everything was upside down.

The monster had him by the ankle and was dangling him over the water. He braced himself to be pulled into the water again or thrown farther out into the ocean.

But to Jordan's surprise, the monster lowered him down gently, right over his grandpa's boat. The monster placed him gingerly on the deck of *The Sea-cret Keeper*.

Then Jordan felt himself being pulled up and fiercely hugged. But he resisted the urge to collapse in his grandpa's arms.

"Tyler . . . Derek . . . Mr. Paxton," he gasped. "We have to do something!"

Captain Joe let go of him and nodded. "Where were they last?" he asked.

Jordan pointed to the tentacles waving in the air. To his surprise, the boys and Mr. Paxton were nowhere to be seen. He looked at his grandpa helplessly.

Captain Joe understood right away. "Look around in the water. See if you can spot them."

Jordan squinted against the spraying ocean water, trying to keep his balance on the wildly swaying boat. Off the starboard side, Jordan thought he saw a flash of a red life jacket.

"Over there!" he shouted, pointing to the bobbing red color. Captain Joe turned the boat in the direction Jordan pointed, and Tyler and Derek came into view. As the boat chugged up to them, Jordan and the captain grabbed their arms and hauled them up. Jordan almost lost his balance and tipped over into the water, but

he caught himself just in time. He noticed the waves weren't quite so choppy now.

Tyler landed with a thump on the boat's deck and panted, "Dad?"

Jordan looked around the ocean, but all he could see was the orange of the monster's huge eye, and the tentacles still waving in the air. A flash of white appeared right next to the eye, and the water calmed down even more.

Tia. Tia had somehow told the monster to take it easy on them. Jordan thought of his grandpa's words: *If you respect things, they will respect you back.*

A shout behind them caught Jordan's attention. Way back toward land, another flash of red bobbed in the water. Jordan could just make out the waving arms of Mr. Paxton.

Captain Joe took one more look at Tia and played the horn just for her. Jordan ran to the front of the boat and yelled, "Thank you! And I'm sorry!"

Then Captain Joe turned the boat around, aiming for the flailing Mr. Paxton. They managed to scoop him up, and Captain Joe sped toward land.

When they arrived at *The Sea-cret Keeper*'s dock, they all dragged themselves off the boat while Captain Joe tied it up. Jordan had never been more grateful to step on land.

Mr. Paxton grabbed Tyler and Derek and hugged them close. "What was that?" he asked Captain Joe, wiping his eyes.

Captain Joe squinted. "That, sir, was the Kraken. A friend of the white dolphin. And he's mighty angry."

Mr. Paxton put his arms around Tyler and Derek. "Thank you for saving our lives," he said, his face still pale. He turned around, pulling his boys with him. Jordan heard him mutter under his breath, "I should have killed that dolphin when I had the chance."

Jordan and Captain Joe looked at each other and shook their heads.

Chapter 8

THE KRAKEN'S REVENGE

"Come on, kid, let's get you inside so you can dry off," Captain Joe said, putting his arm around Jordan.

Jordan took one last look at the sea. The monster seemed to be gone, but the water still rocked and churned. And the sky was still gray and stormy, even though the swirling clouds had disappeared. Although Jordan was on land, he

felt oddly uneasy about taking his eyes off the sea—but he turned around with Captain Joe.

"How did you find us?" Jordan asked as they walked along the boardwalk.

"It was a lucky thing, that," Captain Joe said. "I happened to be checking my boat and tying her down more securely. I saw the skies getting dark and the sea getting restless, so I wanted to secure her. And then I heard the Mayday from Mr. Paxton."

Captain Joe suddenly stopped in the middle of the boardwalk. Then he pulled Jordan into a fierce hug. "I didn't know you were out there, son. I don't know what I would have done if I'd lost you."

Jordan felt tears in his eyes. "Grandpa," he said, "I know why the Kraken came."

Captain Joe let go of Jordan and stood back. "What happened?"

Jordan swallowed. "Yesterday, when we went out on the boat, Mr. Paxton tried to shoot Tia with a harpoon. I didn't say anything. I should have, but I didn't. I pretended to trip and knocked into Mr. Paxton to throw his aim off, but the harpoon still skimmed Tia."

Captain Joe took off his hat and wiped his forehead with the back of his hand. "That was good thinking, son," he said.

Jordan shook his head. "But I should have said something. So that's why I went back today. I told them it was wrong to do what they did. They laughed at me. But I remembered what you said about what the measure of a person is. And I . . . I wanted you to be proud. I wanted to speak up for what's right, to take care of the sea."

Jordan thought he saw a tear travel down a crease in Captain Joe's face. "I think the only reason we're still alive is because you stopped Mr. Paxton from doing any real damage. I think if Tia had been seriously hurt, or worse yet, killed, even I would have been squashed. I can't believe, to tell you the truth, that the Kraken stopped when it did."

Captain Joe paused for a moment and put his hands on Jordan's shoulders. "But anyway, you stood up for what was right," he continued. "And you have made me mighty proud, Jordan. Proudest grandpa there ever was." He wrapped his arms around his grandson again.

At first, Jordan thought it had gotten darker because of the hug. But when his grandpa released him, he realized that the sky had suddenly turned almost as dark as night. The wind picked up and whipped harder against Jordan and Captain Joe. They both turned to the sea.

The swirling clouds were back, but this time much bigger. Lightning flashed all the way through them and struck down on the water. The sea bucked and groaned.

"Grandpa . . . ," Jordan said.

Captain Joe looked as white as a sheet. As they both stood and watched, the sea came rushing toward Cape May's beach.

And then a long, writhing tentacle slammed down in the sand, slithered across the boardwalk, and wriggled down the street toward the Paxtons' house. People screamed and ran.

Another tentacle slammed down on land.

"The Kraken isn't done," Captain Joe said. "It still wants its revenge!"

Jordan watched—terrified—as the Kraken pulled itself on land!

ABOUT THE AUTHOR

Megan Atwood is a writer and professor with more than forty-five books published. She lives in New Jersey, where she wrangles cats, dreams up scary stories, and thinks of ways to keep kids on the edge of their seats.

ABOUT THE ILLUSTRATOR

Neil Evans is a Welsh illustrator. A lifelong comic art fan, he drifted into children's illustration at art college and has since done plenty of both. He enjoyed a few years as a member of various unheard-of indie rock bands (and as a maker of bizarre small press comics), before settling down to get serious about making a living from illustration. He loves depicting emotion, expression, and body language, and he loves inventing unusual creatures and places. When not hunched over a graphics tablet, he can usually be found hunched over a guitar, or dreaming up book pitches and silly songs with his partner, Susannah. They live together in North Wales.

GLOSSARY

boardwalk (BORD-wawk)—a raised wooden walkway along a beach or waterfront

endangered species (in-DAYN-juhrd SPEE-sheez)—a type of animal or plant that is in danger of dying out

first mate (FURST MATE)—a deck officer who is second in command on a ship

harpoon (har-POON)—a long spear with an attached rope that can be thrown or shot to hunt large fish or whales

mantelpiece (MAN-tuhl-peess)—a wooden or stone shelf above a fireplace

Mayday (MAY-day)—a word that is used all over the world to call for help or rescue

tentacle (TEN-tuh-kuhl)—a long, armlike body part some animals use to touch, grab, or smell

throttle (THROT-uhl)—a lever, pedal, or handle used to control the speed of an engine

whirlpool (WURL-pool)—a water current that moves rapidly in a circle

TALK ABOUT IT

1. Jordan didn't want to stay with his grandpa at the
    beginning of the story. Why do you think that was,
    and what eventually changed how he felt about
    Captain Joe?

2. Captain Joe says that if you respect things, they respect
    you back. Describe a time in your life when you found
    that to be true.

3. Why does Captain Joe save Mr. Paxton from the Kraken?
    Do you think he did the right thing?

WRITE ABOUT IT

1. The Kraken is so large, Jordan only sees parts of it at first, such as its huge orange eye and long tentacles. Draw a picture of the whole Kraken and write a paragraph detailing its features and abilities.

2. Imagine that you are a reporter onshore watching the Kraken's attack at sea. Write a newspaper article describing the event.

3. At the end of the story, the Kraken is pulling itself onto shore. Write a new chapter to show what happens next. What does it do to Cape May, and how do the town's citizens escape? You decide!